IDA AND THE
WOOL SMUGGLERS

IDA AND THE W

By Sue Ann Alderson   *Pictures by* Ann Blades

OOL SMUGGLERS

A Meadow Mouse Paperback

Groundwood/Douglas & McIntyre

Vancouver/Toronto

*L*ong ago, when tall trees grew where cities now stand, farmers settled the islands that lie off the west coast of Canada. On one of these island farms Ida lived with her big brother John and her little sister Martha and their mother and father.

There was always lots of work to do, and everybody helped. Neighbors helped each other, too. They built barns together and rounded up sheep together. The neighbors nearest to Ida's family were the Springmans.

One day Ida's mother said after breakfast, "The Springmans' baby came the day before yesterday. Ida, will you take a basket of bread to them this morning? They'll be too busy for baking just yet."

A new baby! Ida loved little babies. When Martha was new, Ida had been too little to hold her, but she'd rocked her to sleep in the wooden cradle. Now Martha was almost too big for the cradle.

"Ida's too little to go to the Springmans' by herself," said John.

"She's the only one who can go," Mother replied. "Your father needs you to help mend the fences, and I have to stay with Martha. She's too heavy for me to carry all that way."

Sometimes it seemed to Ida that she was the only one who wasn't growing and changing.

This year John was big enough to help with the sheep run. Now that it was almost summer, it was nearly time for that. The men and the older boys would line up on both sides of the valley and join in yelling up a fine great noise. Then they would move together, driving the sheep ahead of them into the big corral where the animals would be shorn.

Some of the bigger, stronger girls were allowed to help in the sheep run, but most of the girls and the women packed picnic lunches into boats and rowed around the point to the corral. When the sheep were all rounded up, the families ate together, joking and singing. Usually someone would play the fiddle, and there would be dancing. It was always a grand picnic!

John was lucky, Ida thought. She wished she could help run the sheep. But whenever she asked, her father just smiled and said, "When you're big enough, my girl. When you're big enough."

"Ida, now, will you please take the bread?" Mother asked again.

"It's too dangerous for Ida to go," said John. "Sheep have been stolen these last two weeks, and smugglers will be in the woods looking for strays."

Ida knew about smugglers. Sometimes they stayed in tiny shacks in the woods. They rowed over from the mainland using padded oars so no one could hear them coming and going. They stole sheep, sheared them and then smuggled the wool to the mainland to sell. After the sheep were shorn, they were left to wander about the island. Sometimes a sheep even became a smuggler's dinner—or a cougar's.

"Ida will be safe if she follows the meadow trail and stays away from the woods," said Mother. "The Springmans will need the bread. Ida!" Mother's voice was stern but with a smile in it. "Are you dreaming, girl? Did you hear me say about the Springmans' baby and taking the bread?"

"I'd like to take the bread," Ida said. "I'll walk through the meadow and see Tandy and the lambs." Tandy was Ida's special pet ewe, and this year she had had beautiful twin lambs.

Then Ida thought of a question. "Will Mrs. Springman let me hold the baby?"

"No, probably not," her mother answered. "The Springman baby is too new to be passed around to small children for holding. But I'm sure you'll be able to see him."

Ida was disappointed. But maybe her mother was right. Maybe Ida still wasn't big enough to hold a new baby.

"Here, now," Mother said. "Be careful to stay in the middle of the meadow as you go. If you hear any whistling in the woods it may be smugglers. That's how they signal each other. If you hear a whistle, run straight back here or to the Springmans' to get help."

"I will," said Ida, and she took the basket and set out.

Ida walked through the meadow. When she was more than halfway to the Springmans', she saw Tandy and her lambs grazing by themselves. Most of the sheep were too wild and shy to pet and ran away when Ida came near them, but Tandy was special. She let Ida come right up to her.

Ida gave her a nice scrubbing-sort of petting. "What a lot of itchy wool to wear," she said. "Soon it will be sheep-run time, and then you'll have a haircut and you'll be able to feel the sun and the breezes better."

Tandy's twin lambs watched Ida. Slowly they came a little closer and a little closer, until she could lift her hand slowly and gently stroke their fleecy new coats.

"I have to go now, to take the Springmans this bread," Ida told Tandy and the lambs. "I'll see you later, on my way home."

But just as she started off again, Ida heard a whistle from the woods on one side of the meadow. She stopped and listened. Perhaps it was a bird.

Another whistle came from the other side of the meadow. No. That was not a bird. Then there were two short sharp whistles from the nearer woods and an answer from the other side.

Smugglers! They must be after Tandy and the twins. Ida had to save them, she just had to. But what could she do? Mother had said to run for help if she heard whistling. But then the smugglers would surely steal the sheep. Oh, if only she could take Tandy and the lambs with her.

Again a whistle came from the other side of the meadow. Again there was an answering whistle.

Ida had an idea. She would have her very own sheep run. Quietly, she walked around behind Tandy. Now what noise should she make? She didn't want to scare Tandy so that she would run off into the woods. She just wanted to make her move forward.

Ida thought. When you wanted to move chickens, you said, "Shoo!" When you wanted to move kittens, you said, "Scat!" When you wanted to call pigs, you said "Soo-ey!" Maybe all three together would work for sheep.

Ida tried it.

"Soo-ey! Shoo! Scat!"

And she clapped her hands, *clappety-clap*.

"Soo-ey! Shoo! Scat!"

Clap! Clappety-clap!

And sure enough, Tandy lifted her head and moved off ahead of Ida. After a few steps, she stopped. So Ida tried it again.

"Soo-ey! Shoo! Scat!"

Clap! Clappety-clap!

And Tandy moved again, her lambs following her. It was working! Ida walked behind Tandy and the lambs, herding them a few steps at a time down the meadow.

Sometimes Tandy would trot off to one side. Then Ida had to go after her and shoo her back the right way. It was slow work. Ida grew tired. And she worried about the smugglers. Would they follow her? Would they jump out of the woods and grab Tandy and the lambs and run away? It was better not to think about it.

"Soo-ey! Shoo! Scat!"

Clap! Clappety-clap!

Step by step, Ida drove Tandy and the lambs all the way through the meadow to the Springmans' house.

She told the Springmans about the whistling in the woods.

"You're a clever, brave girl," said Mrs. Springman. "Not many your size could do a sheep run on their own. Next year at the run, you'll go out with the big ones, I'm sure of it."

Mr. Springman hitched up the horse and wagon to drive Ida and Tandy and the twins home. Then he and Ida's father would make sure the smugglers had gone.

"But first," said Mrs. Springman, "I think you might like a picnic. Running sheep is hungry work, and now we have all this lovely bread, thanks to you. Aren't you hungry, Ida? Wouldn't you like a bit to eat?"

All of a sudden Ida felt very hungry indeed.

"Yes, please," she said, "if you have enough."

"That we do," Mrs. Springman replied. "I'll cut that lovely fresh bread and we'll have it with butter and blackberry tea. But I can't set out a picnic and rock a baby to sleep at the same time. Ida, do you think you could hold the baby for me?"

"Yes," said Ida. "I think I'm big enough now."

And she was.

To Angus
A.B.

For Rebecca and Kai,
Ruth and Gene,
Wendy, Steve and Fiona,
with love.
S.A.

Text copyright © 1987 by Sue Ann Alderson
Illustrations copyright © 1987 by Ann Blades

Canadian Cataloguing in Publication Data

Alderson, Sue Ann, 1940-
    Ida and the wool smugglers

ISBN 0-88899-119-3

I. Blades, Ann, 1947-   . II. Title.

PS8551.L34I3 1990   jC813'.54   C90-094045-X
PZ7.A5Id 1990

First paperback edition 1990
Design by Michael Solomon
Printed and bound in Hong Kong by
Everbest Printing Co., Ltd.